buddies
children's thoughts on friendship

buddies
children's thoughts on friendship

Hand-tinted photography
collected and colored by Peggy Lindt

SALT LAKE CITY

First Edition

99 98 97 96 95   10 9 8 7 6 5 4 3 2 1

Text copyright © 1995 by Gibbs Smith, Publisher
All rights reserved.

This is a Peregrine Smith book, published by
Gibbs Smith, Publisher
P.O. Box 667
Layton, Utah 84041

Book design by Mary Ellen Thompson, TTA Design
Hand-tinted photography collected & colored by Peggy Lindt
Dawn Valentine Hadlock, Editor

Printed and bound in Hong Kong

Library of Congress Cataloging-In-Publication Data

Lindt, Peggy.
   Buddies / hand-tinted photography collected and colored by Peggy
Lindt ; text by editorial staff, Gibbs Smith, Publisher.
       p.   cm.
   ISBN 0-87905-663-0
   1. Friendship—Quotations, maxims, etc.—Juvenile literature.
I. Gibbs Smith, Publisher. II. Title.
PN6084.F8L56 1995
177' .6—dc20   94-38602
                                                 CIP
                                                 AC

Credits

Photographs by Peggy Lindt copyright © 1993:

girl with poodle
boy with parrot on head
girl with chicken in basket
cowgirl with orange cat
girl sitting on bench with cat
girl in hammock with puppy
blond boy with white dog
boy feeding carrot to pig

Original black-and-white photographs courtesy of the Los Angeles Public Library, Security Pacific Collections:

girl with donkey
girl's tea party with dog
girl with parakeet and yellow ribbon
girl with horned toad
girl on beach with St. Bernard

All other photographs are stock images.

a buddy . . .

will help carry your load.

a buddy . . .

is somebody to lean on.

a buddy . . .

is happy when you're happy.

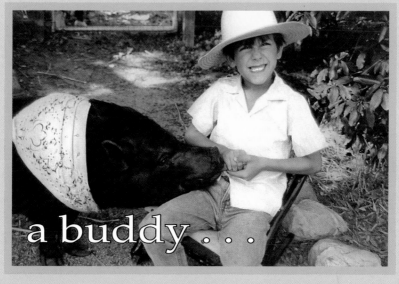

a buddy . . .

knows how to give and take.

a buddy . . .

doesn't mind going along with your whims.

a buddy . . .

doesn't care if you eat too much.

a buddy . . .

will stand by your side.

a buddy . . .

helps you up when you're down.

a buddy . . .

knows how to make you smile.

a buddy . . .

makes you feel cozy and safe.

a buddy . . .

is always ready for adventure.

a buddy . . .

will go anywhere with you.

a buddy . . .

knows how to keep a secret.

a buddy . . .

doesn't care what you look like.

a buddy . . .

makes any day better
just by being there.

a buddy . . .

doesn't run away from a hug.

a buddy . . .

will always come to your party.

a buddy . . .

is somebody to look up to.

a buddy . . .

is kind and gentle.

a buddy . . . .

is somebody to treasure.

a buddy . . .

**can take the words
right out of your mouth.**

a buddy . . .

loves you even when
you're not at your best.

a buddy . . .

is all ears.

a buddy . . .

is somebody who cares.